HIP-HOP

D1307424

-Hop:
t History

a Waters

Crest Publishers

Hip-Hop: A Short History

FRONTIS Hip-hop is more than music—it's a cultu
beyond the dance floor.

PRODUCED BY 21ST CENTURY PUBLISHING AN

EDITORIAL BY HARDING HOUSE PUBLISHING S

MASON CREST PUBLISHERS INC.
370 Reed Road
Broomall, Pennsylvania 19008
(866)MCP-BOOK (toll free)
www.masoncrest.com

Printed in the U.S.A.

Third Printing

9 8 7 6 5 4 3

Library of Congress Cataloging-in-Publication Dat

Waters, Rosa.
   Hip-hop: a short history / by Rosa Waters.
      p. cm. — (Hip-hop)
   Includes bibliographical references (p.   ) and ind
Hardback edition: ISBN-13: 978-1-4222-0109-1
Hardback edition: ISBN-10: 1-4222-0109-0
Paperback edition: ISBN-13: 978-1-4222-0261-6
   1. Rap (Music)—History and criticism—Juvenile I
ML3531.W37 2007
782.42164909—dc22

Publisher's notes:

Contents

Hip-Hop Timeline

1974 Hip-hop pioneer Afrika Bambaataa organizes the Universal Zulu Nation.

1988 *Yo! MTV Raps* premieres on MTV.

1970s Hip-hop as a cultural movement begins in the Bronx, New York City.

1985 *Krush Groove*, a hip-hop film about Def Jam Recordings, is released featuring Run-D.M.C., Kurtis Blow, LL Cool J, and the Beastie Boys.

1970s DJ Kool Herc pioneers the use of breaks, isolations, and repeats using two turntables.

1979 The Sugarhill Gang's song "Rapper's Delight" is the first hip-hop single to go gold.

1986 Run-D.M.C. are the first rappers to appear on the cover of *Rolling Stone* magazine.

1970   1980   1988

1976 Grandmaster Flash & the Furious Five pioneer hip-hop MCing and freestyle battles.

1986 Beastie Boys' album *Licensed to Ill* is released and becomes the best-selling rap album of the 1980s.

1970s Break dancing emerges at parties and in public places in New York City.

1982 Afrika Bambaataa embarks on the first European hip-hop tour.

1988 Hip-hop music annual record sales reaches $100 million.

1970s Graffiti artist Vic pioneers tagging on subway trains in New York City.

1984 *Graffiti Rock*, the first hip-hop television program, premieres.

1993 Rapper Snoop Dogg's album *Doggystyle* is the first debut album to hit the music charts at number one.

2006 Queen Latifah becomes the first hip-hop artist to receive a star on the Hollywood Walk of Fame.

1989 DJ Jazzy Jeff & The Fresh Prince become the first hip-hop artists to win a Grammy Award.

2003 Rapper Eminem becomes the first hip-hop artist to win an Academy Award.

2005 Hip-hop artist Kanye West appears on the cover of *Time* magazine.

1989 Rap is added as a new category to the *Billboard* charts.

1997 East Coast rapper Notorious B.I.G. (aka Biggie Smalls) is murdered.

2004 First National Hip-Hop Political Convention is held in Newark, New Jersey.

1989   2000   2006

1996 West Coast rapper Tupac Shakur is shot and killed.

1990s Hip-hop emerges in Europe.

2005 Rapper Will Smith opens the Philadelphia Live 8 concert as part of 10 simultaneous concerts held worldwide to bring attention to the extreme poverty in Africa.

1989 First gangsta rap album, *Straight Outta Compton*, is released by N.W.A.

2001 The hip-hop political action group, Hip-Hop Summit Action Network, is founded by Russell Simmons.

2006 The Smithsonian Institute National Museum of American History announces the creation of a new hip-hop exhibition scheduled to open in three to five years.

1992 Dr. Dre's album *The Chronic* is released; it redefines West Coast rap.

Slaves brought from Africa tried hard to keep parts of their culture alive. Among these were traditions of dance and music. Hip-hop is just one form of music and dance that can trace its beginnings to the many cultures of those slaves from Africa.

1

The Roots of Hip-Hop

Life is full of rhythms. The tap-tap-tap of heels on the sidewalk . . . the drip-drip of rain on the roof . . . the slap-slap of windshield wipers . . . the ka-thud, ka-thud of a beating heart . . . the rise and fall of kids' voices in school hallways. These rhythms surround us every day. Most of the time, we barely notice.

But hip-hop musicians pay attention to these ordinary rhythms. They exaggerate them and weave them through their music in a technique known as rapping. And when we listen to hip-hop, the rhythms get in our muscles, making our legs jump and our toes tap in time. Turn the music up loud enough, and you'll feel as though even the blood in your veins is pumping to the beat!

Born Out of Slavery

Hip-hop is America's very own music, a unique art form produced by the mixture of cultures brought together, one way or another, within the

United States. Hip-hop's earliest and deepest roots, however, stretch across the Atlantic Ocean and dig into the soil of Africa.

Slavery was a cruel and terrible **institution** that tried to turn human beings into objects. But the people who were brought to America as slaves refused to give up their humanity. One way they clung to their identity and dignity was through music. While they worked in the fields, while they cooked and cleaned for rich white folks, they recognized the rhythms of their movements—and they sang to the beat of their bodies' labor. They clapped their hands together, they beat their feet on the ground, and they shouted out the stories of their lives. They sang about freedom, about going home, about sorrows and trials, and their music helped them rise above the pain. While one person sang, those who were working nearby felt free to chime in with their two cents as well. This **spontaneous** music was an ever-changing, living thing, created by the entire community.

As the years went by, the slaves adapted to their new lives, but in their hearts, they never completely lost touch with Africa, the home that had shaped them. Most slaves converted to Christianity, but they made this faith uniquely their own. Rhythm was a part of their worship, and preaching and singing blended together.

The Rhythm of Worship

As the years went by, and African Americans at last gained their freedom, they still listened to life's beat. At black churches, ministers used a preaching form known as "call-and-response." For example, a minister might shout out, "People, can I hear an amen?" and the congregation shouted back, "Amen!"

Martin Luther King Jr., the great African American minister who led the **civil rights movement** in the 1960s, spoke of "singing the Word"; like many other black preachers, King used both melody and rhythm to move his audiences. The voices of black ministers rose and fell, the pitch of their voices creating a beat that could suddenly burst into song. At the same time, black gospel singers might break into a **testimony** in the middle of singing, or the preacher might weave his preaching through the singers' music. Within African American churches, music, spoken words, and rhythm flowed together seamlessly.

But African American music wasn't kept inside church walls. It flowed out into the streets and dance halls. Eventually, talented

Church has always been important to African Americans. Many popular singers, including hip-hop artists, got their starts as members of a church choir. Gospel music has also influenced other styles of music, including R&B and soul.

musicians made it so famous that it started entire new forms of American music.

Rhythm and Blues

The "blues" was a form of music that came directly from the slaves' spirituals, "field hollers," shouts, and chants. It was a form of music that gave voice to life's sorrow. In the 1940s, this music combined with jazz

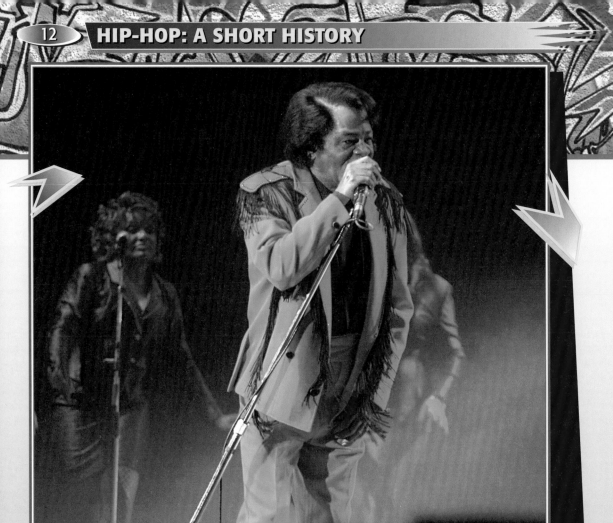

Born and raised amid poverty and segregation, James Brown used his voice to give hope to others with similar backgrounds. His many nicknames—"Soul Brother Number One," "The Godfather of Soul," and "the Godfather of Hip-Hop"—show his influence and importance on the music scene.

(another form of African American music that had become popular across the United States in the 1920s). Rhythm and blues—or R&B—was the child of the marriage between blues and jazz. Eventually, this style of music would grow up to be rock and roll. Drummers played an important role in the development of this music.

Beating Out the Rhythm

Drummer Earl Palmer grew up in New Orleans and later moved to Los Angeles, leaving his mark on the music scenes in both cities in the 1950s. He had a powerful backbeat and mastery of "shuffle" rhythms. (A "shuffle" is a pair of repeated notes, where the emphasis on the first beat is exaggerated, while the second is lessened in emphasis.) Palmer's first love was jazz, but his fast stick work and backbeats made their way into the music of the 1960s.

Clyde Stubblefield was another drummer who helped lay the foundation for a new sound in music. Born in 1943, he started his musical career as a child in Chattanooga, Tennessee, where he played on tin can lids, cardboard boxes, and anything else that would make a sound. As an adult, he played all over the world—and his rhythm influenced some of the greatest performers, including James Brown.

The Godfather of Hip-Hop

James Brown was born in 1933 in the Deep South in the midst of the **Depression**; poverty was everywhere, and things were even worse for African Americans, especially in the South, where blacks were strictly **segregated**. But James found a way for blacks to rise above their circumstances.

During the 1960s, soul music became popular, a combination of gospel and rhythm and blues that merged together religious and **secular** themes. The word "soul" also became a symbol of pride and identity for African Americans. And James Brown became known as "Soul Brother Number One." His hit recordings—with titles like "Say It Loud—I'm Black and I'm Proud" (1968)—marked the beginning of a new movement. For the first time, African Americans held their heads high and asserted, "Black is beautiful!" Across America, Brown was a spokesperson for this movement.

The way James Brown blended together blues, gospel, jazz, and country vocal styles made him one of the most influential vocalists of the twentieth century—but James Brown didn't just sing. He also danced with his microphone, he made acrobatic leaps with full-impact knee landings, and his feet beat out the rhythm of his music. His extraordinary sense of timing was expressed in his skill as both a dancer and singer. As a result, he brought rhythm to the foreground of popular music. His influence inspired yet another new form of American music—funk.

Funk Music

Compared to the 1960s' soul music, funk typically uses more complex rhythms, while the melodies are usually simpler. Often, the structure of a funk song consists of just one or two riffs (short, musical phrases). Where one riff changes to another often becomes the highlight of a song. Funk music was meant for dancing, and its goal was to create as intense a groove as possible. One of its most distinctive features was the role played by bass guitars, which never before had played so loudly. The groundwork was laid for the first beats of hip-hop.

The DJs Who Made It Happen

Clive Campbell came from Jamaica to New York City's South Bronx when he was twelve years old. He was a big kid, and as he grew older, he earned the name Hercules—which eventually, as he became famous for the musical parties he DJed, turned into "Kool Herc."

Today, Herc and another DJ, D.J. Hollywood, are credited with being the first to introduce a Jamaican style of music—cutting and mixing—to the South Bronx. Herc is said to be the first person to use two copies of the same record to turn a fifteen-second segment into a piece of music that went on and on, mixing back and forth between the two records, using the turntables as musical instruments to create a new sound that changed America's music scene forever.

While Herc was performing with turntables, he was also **emceeing**, using his microphone to mix in jokes, boasts, and other comments. Herc's musical parties became more famous when they were recorded on cassette tapes that were passed around the Bronx, Brooklyn, and uptown Manhattan, allowing other DJs to imitate his style.

Afrika Bambaataa, a Black Muslim, was one of the most important of these DJs. He and Herc had a friendly competition: they held sound system competitions in city parks, where they hot-wired street lamps for electricity. Bambaataa mixed in sounds from rock music recordings and even television shows, adding his own creativity to Herc's original sound.

Other DJs and rappers came along—Grandmaster Flash, the Last Poets, and Grandmaster Caz with the Cold Crush Brothers, among others—and each built and embellished Herc's original styles. Grandmaster Flash invented the technique called "cutting," and Grandmaster Caz was the first to incorporate spoken rhymes

The early days of hip-hop didn't rely on voices. DJ and emcee Kool Herc turned the turntable into an instrument. DJs such as Grandmaster Flash, shown here working the turntables, introduced techniques such as "cutting" and "scratching" the vinyl records into the performance.

with the music that came from the turntables. The Lost Poets used hip-hop to express a political message.

Hip-hop offered urban black youth a voice that was uniquely their own. It was a fresh, flexible sound that could stretch and expand in any direction they needed—and no white man's rules held them back. Hip-hop could swear; it could tell crude jokes; it could express anger and frustration; and it could make them proud to be themselves.

But hip-hop was far more than just music. It soon became an entire culture that included its own language, fashion, values, politics, perspectives—and images. Graffiti was the visual expression of hip-hop.

Graffiti

In the early 1970s, a mail courier named Vic set a goal for himself: he would ride every subway and bus in New York City. To keep track of his progress, he wrote his name and courier number (156) on each train and bus he rode. Meanwhile, a young messenger named Demetrius, who lived on 183rd Street in New York, was leaving his mark on the outsides and insides of subway cars: Taki 183. Kids all over the city, realizing the fame they could gain by "tagging" their names, set themselves their own goals: to "get up"—to have their name—in as many places as possible.

Soon, graffiti became more than simple tagging. Graffiti writers set themselves higher goals than merely getting their name around as much as possible. Now, they tried to outdo each other with new styles: bubble, wild style, and computer style were just a few of the graffiti techniques invented by taggers like Case 2, Chain 3, Frank 207, and Tracy 168. Taggers added more colors and special effects; they wrote their names bigger and bolder. Tagging reinforced their sense of identity and pride. "We are here," their graffiti shouted, "and we are cool!"

Spray paint allowed large pieces of graffiti to be created fairly quickly. (After all, taggers didn't want to get caught by the police or the Metropolitan Transit Authority.) From simple tags on the insides of trains to masterpieces that spanned multiple cars, graffiti exploded on the subways of New York City. The Ex-Vandals, Wanted, and other graffiti crews worked in groups. Eventually, graffiti artists known as Cornbread and Cool Earl brought the craze to Philadelphia.

Hip-hop is more than music—it is a culture. Part of the cultural expression is through graffiti. Subway cars were favorite targets for graffiti artists. What began as "tagging" something just with initials or a symbol became an art form of complex, colorful images.

Some people see graffiti as a symbol of urban decay—but for the hip-hop culture, graffiti provided the visual inspiration that encouraged other forms of creativity and expression, such as emceeing and DJing. Some of today's best hip-hop artists grew up surrounded by graffiti; and meanwhile, they were also learning the moves of the best b-boys.

Break Dancing

When Kool Herc DJed, he extended the "breaks" or "get-down" sections—the parts where the percussion was the strongest—for as long as possible by using two turntables with double copies of the same record. The dancers who rocked out on the dance floor to the rhythm of these "breakbeats" became known as break-boys or b-boys; later still, they would be known as break-dancers. Their earliest moves—called

Break-dancers entertained club crowds during "get-down" sections of the music. Martial arts and Latino dances added their influences to the "drop" and "in and out" moves. Before long, crowds on the streets were introduced to these young people spinning their bodies in almost unbelievable ways.

the "drop" and the "in and out"—were influenced not only by the music's beat but by moves found in Asian martial arts and Latino dances. The new form of dancing quickly caught on, and the Plaza Tunnel and the Puzzle were two of the first break-dance clubs.

Graffiti gave visual expression to hip-hop culture; emceeing and DJing produced the music; and b-boying was the dance. In hip-hop's early days, all these elements were woven tightly together. Graffiti artists were often b-boys, emcees, and DJs as well. At the South Bronx parties, writers did their things on a wall, a DJ spun and scratched, and the emcee revved up the crowd. And meanwhile, the b-boys "battled" each other on the dance floor. Hip-hop in all its forms provided creative outlets for urban kids whose lives were often frustrating and difficult. It told them, "Your voice can be heard. Your name counts. Your rhythm is powerful."

Former gang leader Afrika Bambaataa (right, in 2005) organized a group of hip-hop pioneers into the Universal Zulu Nation. The group was involved in community activities as well as hip-hop music. More recent hip-hop artists are carrying on this tradition of social activism.

2

Growing Strong

Hip-hop's fresh burst of creativity was too strong to stay within the streets of the South Bronx. Before long, this brash new culture spread across the country, all the way to California, where artists like Lackatron Jon and Shabba-doo added their rhythm. As hip-hop's voice grew louder yet, the East Coast and the West Coast became rivals.

Unfortunately, sometimes this rivalry led to violence and even murder. Despite this, the hip-hop culture was growing up, becoming more organized, more purposeful . . . and even more cool.

Zulu Nation

In 1974, Afrika Bambaataa (also known as Bam), who had once been the leader of a gang called the Black Spades, organized a collective of DJs, graffiti artists, and breakers. Bam wanted to use hip-hop to build awareness of social issues. He called his organization the Universal Zulu

Nation, after the South African tribe that became an empire under the leadership of Shaka Zulu, one of the greatest of the Zulu chieftains. The five b-boys who joined Bam were known as the Shaka Zulu Kings.

The Zulu Nation eventually defined its mission this way:

"As we are dedicated to improving and uplifting ourselves and our communities, all Zulu Nation members should be involved in some activity that is positive and gives back to the community. Hip-Hop music is our vehicle of expression. We can learn to write, produce, market, promote, publish, perform and televise our own music, for our own people. There are too many divisions between males and females. There are too many divisions between young adults and their parents and too many divisions between rich and poor-urban and suburban. Now is the time for us to build together as well as develop individually. All of the ills and problems that plague our community, we are going to address."

Some of the Zulu Nation's community activities included neighborhood cleanups, block parties, talent showcases, seminars, conferences, canned-food drives, and tutoring and mentor programs. Hip-hop was no longer just an angry voice shouting out the frustration of gang members and other urban youths. For the first (but not the last) time, it had become a conscious force for good in urban communities.

The First Hip-Hop Records

By the final years of the 1970s, graffiti crews were "bombing" buildings, cars, street fixtures, and of course the subway with their bold spray-paint illustrations; break-dancers had moved from concrete parks to the wooden floors of clubs like Sparkle, Savoy Manor Ballroom, Ecstasy Garage, T-Connection, and Club 371; and emcee/DJ crews like the Cold Crush Brothers, the Treacherous Three, and the Funky Four + One had developed a smooth, show-biz style. But this brand-new world of music was still completely spontaneous; the only recordings were live **bootleg** tapes that were passed around from boom box to boom box.

MUSIC ALIVE!

Bringing Today's Music to the Classroom

Hail to HIP-HOP!

PLUS

JESSICA SIMPSON
COPYRIGHTS
MUSIC IN PERU

BIRTH OF OLD SCHOOL

One of the first groups to cut a hip-hop record was Sugarhill Gang. In 2004, *Music Alive!* magazine acknowledged the 25th anniversary of the release of the group's *Rapper's Delight* with their picture on its cover and a story on hip-hop in the classroom.

The Fatback Band and the Sugarhill Gang were the first rappers to actually release records. Overnight, Sugar Hill Records became a success—and the b-boys finally heard *their* music on the radio. It wasn't the "real thing," though, in their estimation—but it made them think. As Grandmaster Flash asked, "What power do Sugar Hill have to get something like that on the radio and we can't get ours on it? Ours sounds better than theirs." The rappers got busy. Suddenly, everyone was making singles.

Meanwhile, mainstream America was hearing hip-hop on their radios for the first time. Pop culture had been dancing to disco during the '70s, but it was ready for something new. At first, hip-hop was considered "black" music; white audiences didn't "get" the sound, and they even booed and threw things when rap artists performed. But as the '80s came along, and hip-hop was heard more and more often on radios, it traveled out of the inner cities.

Record companies caught on to the **grassroots** movement and tried to buy it up. They didn't always comprehend, though, that their motivations were not the same as the rappers'. Record companies want to make money, so as the years went by, they signed on the big hip-hop voices—Public Enemy, Boogie Down Productions, Ice T, Paris—but they didn't understand that these folks were angry with the established culture. Rappers wanted to use their music to express that anger, to talk about things like police brutality, black rights, and unfair politics. By definition, hip-hop had never been censored. Meanwhile, the record companies didn't want to make waves or get in trouble. This led to conflicts between the big music companies and the musicians.

The Growth of the Dance Movement

While hip-hop's music was spreading out across America's airways, break-dancing was also making itself known. Charlie Robot introduced "Robot" moves to the mainstream media with his appearance on the TV show *Soul Train*. New b-boy groups formed: Breakmachine, Uprock, Motor City Crew, the Dynamic Rockers, the Rock Steady Crew, Floormasters Incredible Breakers, the Magnificent Force, and many others. California's dance troupes—Campbellockers and Chain Reaction—introduced upright moves like locking, popping, and the electric boogaloo. A few b-girls began stepping out as well: Headspin Janet, Lady Doze, and Daisy "Baby Love" Castro. They dressed like the guys, in windbreakers, Lee jeans, and Adidas sneakers with fat laces.

Hip-hop made its way to television and film, and its influence could not be ignored. It became a category for many music and video awards. Here, Crazy Legs and Rock Steady Crew—pioneers in hip-hop dance—are shown at the 2005 VH1 *Hip-Hop Honors*.

As with the rest of the hip-hop culture, competition was always at the forefront of break-dancing. "What makes it all real," said Kid Freeze in *The Vibe History of Hip Hop*, "is the battle. That's where you see the real chemistry of hip hop." Out of this competition, reputations were built, friendships forged, and enemies made. The break-dance battles weren't always constructive—but they were a lot better than the violence that sometimes broke out in reaction to hip-hop's competitive spirit.

Hip-Hop's Rise

White America couldn't ignore what was going on. TV talk show hosts like Merv Griffin and Dave Letterman asked b-boys to come on their

The turntable and the DJ continue to be important in hip-hop. Here, DJ Grand Master Theodore prepares to entertain the crowd with his emceeing, mixing, cutting, and scratching skills. Hip-hop is no longer confined to the New York streets and clubs—it's everywhere.

shows. Funky Four + One More performed on NBC's *Saturday Night Live.* The movies *Breakin'* and *Breakin' 2: Electric Boogaloo* brought break-dancing to the big screen, as did *Wild Style,* with the Cold Crush Brothers (produced by Fab 5 Freddy and Chris Stein); *Flashdance* with Rock Steady Crew; and *Breakin' and Enterin'* with Shabba Doo, Boogaloo Shrimp, Pop 'n' Taco, Ice-T, Egyptian Lover, and Blue City Strutters. *Beat Street* featured Kool Herc himself, as well as Doug E. Fresh and Kool Moe Dee; the movie highlighted a famous b-boy battle at the Roxy club with Rock Steady Crew and the NYC Breakers.

White musicians—including the Beastie Boys and Blondie's Debbie Harry—were inspired by hip-hop and imitated the sound in their own music. When Michael Jackson moonwalked at the Grammys, break-dancing hit the global scene, and Lionel Richie followed up with his performance at the closing ceremony for the 1984 Olympics. Michael Holman (manager of the NYC Breakers) created the first hip-hop television show, *Graffiti Rock,* which featured special guests like Run-D.M.C., Kool Moe Dee, and Special K.

Meanwhile, the rappers were busy adding their own creative spice to the hip-hop mixture. Afrika Bambaataa introduced the sound of synthesizers and electric drum machines on his 1982 album, *Planet Rock.* DJ Grand Wizard Theodore started "scratching" rhythmic patterns on the records, and Grandmaster Melle made extended storytelling a part of rap.

The electronic sampler allowed any sound to be reproduced and manipulated. Drummed breaks and pieces of old records could be cut up, edited, and put back together. Some people said this was stealing; other people said it was really a new form of creativity. After all, even Shakespeare, one of the most creative minds of all time, borrowed bits and pieces from other works and put them together in brand-new ways. Hip-hop did the same thing: everything rappers saw and heard and touched, flowed out from them in their own original rhythms. They took the established culture and pulled it into pieces, flipped it on its side, and reassembled it to reflect their own personalities. Nothing was beyond their reach. For the first time, African American culture was standing up proud and claiming American culture for itself.

Run-D.M.C. was the first hip-hop group to be shown regularly on MTV, meaning they—and hip-hop—had entered the music mainstream. Shown left to right are "Run" Simmons, "Jam Master Jay" Mizell, and "DMC" McDaniels on their way to the 2002 MTV Music Awards.

3

Going Mainstream

After only a few years, hip-hop culture was transformed from an aspect of a small urban **subculture** to a mainstream music **genre**. Everything from soft drink commercials to white pop music made hip-hop its own. Hip-hop had come a long way from the streets of New York's South Bronx.

In 1986, the Beastie Boys' rap single "(You Gotta) Fight for Your Right (To Party!)" moved to the top ten on the *Billboard* charts, and an Aerosmith song, "Walk This Way," performed with rapper group Run-D.M.C., joined it. The first major female rap group, Salt-N-Peppa, released the single "Push It," which made it to the top twenty on the *Billboard* charts. Run-D.M.C. became one of the first rap groups to be featured regularly on MTV, and Spike Lee's 1989 movie, *Do the Right Thing*, brought hip-hop to everyone's attention.

"Pop Rap"

Some hip-hop artists felt that by creating a version of rap music that was suited for popular media, the real hip-hop had been watered down and sterilized. Hip-hop was supposed to be spontaneous, original, and ever new—but how could it be those things when it was being mass-produced for mainstream culture? When MC Hammer covered the Chi-Lites' "Have You Seen Her," for instance, it was nearly a note-for-note duplication of the original, rather than the kaleidoscope of sound and rhythm that Kool Herc would have produced for the dance floor. What's more, ghetto rappers were often a little too rough and real for popular consumption, so some of them sanded off their bumps and made themselves smoother for the commercial world.

The old hip-hop fans weren't sure what to make of the new pop rap. The tension came to a head at a club performance by P.M. Dawn, where KRS-One and a posse of fans stormed the stage and yanked the microphone away from P.M. Dawn's Prince Be. According to *The Vibe History of Hip Hop*, KRS-One claimed that this was "the first time a believed-to-be-hardcore artist took a physical reaction to a believed-to-be-commercial artist."

Some hip-hoppers also resented white musicians trespassing on their territory. These white musicians didn't come from the same deprived background, so what gave them the right to hip-hop's anger and drive? What's more, they didn't even always understand the vocabulary.

The Beastie Boys were the exception. They managed to make hip-hop their own without offending the African American community. Black rapper Q-Tip said of the Beastie Boys: "They don't try to be black. They're just themselves—not trying to be something else."

While black rap musicians respected the Beastie Boys' originality, however, they didn't feel the same about rapper Vanilla Ice. Vanilla Ice seemed determined to "use" hip-hop to make himself rich. Even worse, his success inspired other white performers to follow in his footsteps. "Marky Mark" Wahlberg, for example, burst onto the charts and MTV with his 1991 hit, "Good Vibrations," but the white ghetto image he cultivated was rudely shattered when the news broke that he had been involved in a racially motivated assault.

Still, hip-hop's goal has always been to suck in the biggest possible audience; that's what Kool Herc was all about at the very beginning. None of the early rappers were opposed to making money, either. And some hip-hop musicians managed to cross the line between grassroots and mainstream without losing their integrity. Sean "Puffy" Combs (or Puff Daddy or P. Diddy, or just plain Diddy) was one of these artists. Puff Daddy's success turned him into a sort of ghetto superhero, a star who was appreciated by both mainstream America and hip-hop's inner-city roots.

MTV and Hip Hop

MTV was slow to include black artists, let alone black hip-hop artists, in its videos. In 1983, the *New York Times* noted, "The program can be watched for hours at a time without detecting the presence of a single black performer." According to *Rolling Stone* magazine, of the 750

When hip-hop entered the mainstream, white artists joined in, much to the anger of some hip-hop originators. One group—the Beastie Boys—did have the respect of many hip-hop artists. Why? They weren't trying to be black.

music videos MTV showed during its first eighteen months on the air, fewer than two dozen featured black artists.

At first, MTV even refused to play superstar Michael Jackson's videos; the music and visual content was said to be "inappropriate" for their viewers. Finally, CBS Records president Walter Yetnikoff is said to have phoned MTV's CEO and told him if he refused to play Michael Jackson's "Billie Jean," MTV would get no more videos from CBS artists. Jackson's video was reluctantly accepted—and sales for his album *Thriller* made music history.

What's more, Michael Jackson opened up MTV for other black musicians, including Prince, Run-D.M.C., the Fat Boys, Salt-N-Peppa, DJ Jazzy Jeff, the Fresh Prince—and eventually, even Public Enemy. MTV with its music videos gave hip-hop back its strong visual overtones; now people could *see* the moves and the style.

Hip-Hop Commercials

Just as MTV had been slow to jump on the hip-hop wagon, the advertising world also was leery of rap music. After all, its performers tended to be angry and rebellious—and anger and rebellion aren't usually big sellers for mainstream America. However, in the 1980s all that began to change.

For the most part, rock-and-roll musicians had never particularly embraced **consumerism**, but many hip-hop artists weren't afraid to make a buck any way they could—and after their poverty-stricken childhoods, material goods delighted them. Run-D.M.C., for example, just loved Adidas, and they had no problem telling the world they did in their music. The Fat Boys liked to rhyme about their favorite food products, and L.L. Cool J dropped so many brand names into his album *Bigger and Deffer* that advertisers finally caught on.

Kurtis Blow signed on with Coke; Kool Moe Dee and the Fresh Prince represented Mountain Dew; and of course, Run-D.M.C. was only too happy to hawk Adidas. Commercials reach into every home with a television—which meant that hip-hop was now firmly a part of the American consciousness.

As a result, in 1988, the annual record sales of hip-hop music reached $100 million. The next year, *Billboard* added rap charts to its magazine, and MTV debuted *Yo!MTV Raps*, which soon became the network's highest-rated show. Hip-hop musicians were making money and gaining popularity—but that didn't mean that many of them

A major hurdle hip-hop artists had to conquer to be accepted by America was getting MTV to show their videos. Videos by any black musician—even superstar Michael Jackson—were scarce on MTV. Here's Michael doing his moonwalk at the 1995 MTV Video Music Awards.

weren't also doing what hip-hop had always done best: shouting out the truth, no matter how ugly.

Women Find a Place

Males have always dominated hip-hop, while women's roles in rap music usually placed them out of the spotlight as back-up singers or dancers. At

Women in early hip-hop were generally seen only as dancers or back-up singers. The first important female rap group was Salt-N-Pepa, shown here (left to right: DJ Spinderella [Deirdre Roper], Cheryl "Salt" James, and Sandy "Pepa" Denton). They helped open doors for other female musicians.

the end of the 1980s, however, for the first time, women rappers gained recognition and respect. Female rap groups used powerful lyrics to argue against our society's traditional roles for women; they demanded equal treatment for women and called on women to support each other. Popular female rappers like Salt-N-Peppa and Monie Love work to give all women, especially African American women, a strong sense of self-identity and empowerment.

True to Their Roots

In the 1980s, a large piece of the rap scene became very political, and performers used their music to communicate their message. This trend has carried on through today. Hip-hop music has a social **agenda**, one that is louder and more open than any popular music had carried since the peace movement of the 1960s.

Groups like Public Enemy and Boogie Down represented rap's political style. *It Takes a Nation of Millions to Hold Us Back*, Public Enemy's second album, shot the group into fame. According to the group's lead singer, Chuck D., hip-hop was far more than entertainment. For black American culture, rap was equivalent to the white world's CNN (Cable News Network): it was the way ideas and events were communicated.

But that has always been true of African Americans' music. All the way back to slavery's evil reign, music has risen up from the black community, beating out the rhythm of truth and freedom. African American music is a private language that will never be silenced. But now, the whole world is hearing it.

Hip-hop has spread far beyond the shores of its birthplace. Today, countries all over the world have their own rap stars, and American artists perform concerts throughout the world. Here, Pharrell Williams is shown with Japanese rappers at a 2005 concert in Tokyo.

Hip-Hop Around the World

Music videos and international broadcasting on the MTV channel meant that hip-hop spread rapidly around the world. Young people outside the United States could easily relate to hip-hop's themes, and cultures around the world adopted and adapted aspects of hip-hop to make it their own.

European Hip-Hop

When Afrika Bambaataa traveled to France in the early 1980s, he was impressed by the presence there of African and Caribbean culture. He encouraged black French youth to use the hip-hop movement to express themselves and affirm their identity. After his visit, break dance was the first element of hip-hop to appear on Europe's public scene, followed by small underground organizations starting to hold rap concerts. At first, European teens were simply imitating Americans, rapping in English, but they soon began using their own languages and making their own cultural **innovations**.

By the 1990s, hip-hop was established in Europe. In England, hip-hop was absorbed by the "club scene" and was transformed into a pop form know as "trip-hop." Groups like US3, Tricky, and Massive Attack were at the forefront of the trip-hop scene. Across the English Channel, in France, French lyrics were laid on top of traditional break beats and elaborate samples from other records. MC Solaar was the first hip-hop star to emerge there.

The English group US3 played an important role in creating "trip-hop," a pop style of hip-hop, popular in clubs across England. Like artists in other countries, trip-hop added elements to traditional hip-hop that made it uniquely their own.

MC Solaar (shown here performing at a 2004 concert in Paris) is a popular rap artist in France. His music is more poetic and lacks the violence that can be found in some American rap.

MC Solaar (whose real name is Claude M'Barali) was born in Senegal to parents who came from the African nation of Chad. The family moved to a suburb of Paris when Claude was still a baby, and he grew up in France. He released a single in 1990, followed soon by two albums, including *Prose Combat,* which is his best known. Both of his albums went **platinum**. His music and lyrics lack the violence that sometimes characterizes American hip-hop; instead, his songs are complex and poetic, built around word play, **philosophical** thoughts, and intricate dance rhythms. He gained fans in North America in 2004, when one of his songs was featured on the television series *Sex and the City*.

After MC Solaar's success, many other French hip-hop bands emerged, followed by a rash of independent record labels. Everyone was looking to create their own version of the French superstar, and rap adapted to the European cultural scene. Alliance Ethnik is another French hip-hop group that has achieved international recognition.

Meanwhile, in Switzerland, Unik Records produced the multicultural rap band Sens Unik, which featured many languages in its music. Nearby, in Belgium, Benny B created a pop version of hip-hop. In Italy, musician Jovanotti started the Italian rap movement, which spoke out loudly against the Italian Mafia. In Sweden, hip-hop artists Just D and Infinite Mass won the Swedish version of the Grammys in 1996; and in Holland, Urban Dance Squad was one of the first bands to rap in Europe. DJAX records, a Dutch rap independent label, promoted Dutch hip-hop artists Extince and Osdorp Posse. And next door in Germany, rap artists were finding their own sound, and independent record labels like Yo Mama, Mzee, and Groove Attack developed local talents with international appeal.

Turkish Hip-Hop

Immigrants from Turkey to Germany grabbed onto hip-hop's voice, allowing it to give expression to their own feelings of **alienation** and frustration with the predominantly white German culture. Groups like Islamic Force and Cartel mixed hip-hop's distinctive sounds with elements of Near Eastern music to create what they call "Oriental Hip-Hop." In 1992, Islamic Force released their first single, "My Melody," followed by a full-length CD, *Mesaj*. DJ Mahmut and Murat G, a hip-hop duo from Frankfurt, Germany, rap in a mixture of German and Turkish, using music from East and West. Founded in the early 1990s, the group has also created their own label, Looptown, on which they put out the Turkish-German rap compilation *Looptown Presents Turkish Hip Hop* (1994), followed by their own album *Garip Dünya* (1997).

New Zealand's Hip-Hop

The native people of New Zealand, the Maori, identify with hip-hop's messages of freedom and justice. Some of the first Maori hip-hop stars

The Maori influenced many of New Zealand's rap artists. Their style of hip-hop—Urban Pasifika—combines traditional rap beats with Maori language and instruments like the ukulele. Scribe (center) is the country's best-known rapper. P-Money (right) is a major hip-hop producer in New Zealand.

include Dalvanius Prime (who created the first New Zealand rap hit single, "Poi E") and Upper Hutt Posse (whose 1988 album *E Tu* was the first New Zealand album of pure hip-hop). The members of Upper Hutt Posse became known for their fierce lyrics in support of Maori **sovereignty**. Many white New Zealanders, however, hated hip-hop, and some radio stations implemented a "no rap, no crap" policy. Despite this, Upper Hutt Posse's DJ, DLT, began the influential radio show *True Skool Hiphop Show*, which joined the *Wednesday Night Jam* in promoting hip-hop. Hip-hop artists—like Rough Opinion, the Wanderers, Temple Jones, and Hamofide—rose to the level of super heroes within the Maori subculture. By the 1990s, Maori as well as other **Polynesian** hip-hop musicians had formed a style known as Urban Pasifika, which combines American-style rap beats with Maori language rhymes and Pacific Island instruments like the ukulele. These artists include Che Fu, Nesian Mystik, and Scribe (who topped both the single and album charts in 2004); P-Money is the biggest New Zealand hip-hop record producer.

As hip-hop has developed here and abroad, it has joined with other influences, creating such new music forms as reggaeton, a combination of hip-hop and Caribbean reggae. Zion and Lenox are popular reggaeton artists, shown here at Reggaeton Festival in 2005.

A Global Voice

Hip-hop has traveled a long way from the streets of the South Bronx. In the twenty-first century, hip-hop's rhythms are heard in Japan, the Dominican Republic, African nations, the Philippines, Puerto Rico . . . and many other countries around the world. New **fusions** have been created, like "reggaeton," which combines hip-hop rhythm with the Caribbean's reggae-style music; "mererap," which blends hip-hop and merengue, a Dominican ballroom dance music; and "Bongo Flava," a marriage of hip-hop with Tanzanian folk music.

While the rest of the world started out imitating America, cultures around the globe have now created their own unique hip-hop versions—and yet by doing so, they remain true to the originality and creativity that are central to hip-hop's deepest and oldest roots. European voices are now influencing American artists as well. For instance, the German band Kraftwerk (which means "power force" in German) has inspired American rappers like Afrika Bambaataa, Grandmaster Flash, Planet Patrol, Jonzun Crew, and Newcleus.

By the twenty-first century, hip-hop has become a truly global voice for independence and creativity. For many minority cultures around the world, it is a powerful and sharp-edged tool for solidarity and self-respect, a voice that has the strength to speak out against injustice in any shape.

Superstar Sean "Diddy" Combs is a major force in convincing hip-hop artists and fans to get educated, vote, and get involved in their communities. These programs reflect the far reach of hip-hop culture in the United States.

5

Hip-Hop and Modern Culture

Hip-hop has always been a **collage** of rhythm, voice, images, and movement. Today's hip-hop culture continues to cross boundaries, binding together ideas, genres, and culture into a new mix. It is a democratic movement: anyone can participate; there is no hierarchy that sets the standards. From politics to urban crime, from fashion to religion, from violence to charity, hip-hop both reflects and shapes modern culture.

Hip-Hop and Politics

In June 2004, the National Hip-Hop Political Convention was held in Newark, New Jersey. Its organizers wanted an opportunity to communicate with the older civil rights movement leaders, looking for ideas and inspiration for using music to bring about positive political change. They wanted to encourage young adults to vote and get involved in politics; most of all, they wanted to make hip-hop a visible presence and an audible voice in America's political arena.

There are many items on hip-hop's political agenda: juvenile justice; equal rights for all races, including both African and Native Americans; urban renewal; poverty; homelessness; police violence—to name just a few. Lyrics are just one way these causes are given voice; hip-hop artists are also outspoken and courageous in their confrontation with America's political system.

After Hurricane Katrina ravaged America's Gulf Region, hip-hop artist Kanye West, one of the narrators for an NBC special, "Concert for Hurricane Relief," startled viewers with his ad-lib comments. "I hate the way they portray us in the media," he said, referring to the media's portrayal of African Americans in New Orleans. "If you see a black family it says they are looting; if you see a white family it says they are looking for food." He went on to say, "George Bush doesn't care about black people." Across America, **conservatives** were outraged, while many **liberals** were delighted by West's daring. But Kanye West was simply doing what hip-hop has always done: speaking the truth, as he saw it, without apology or censorship.

Hip-hop **activist** William Upski Wimsatt is trying to create a national voting bloc of young people. "A hip-hop mind is an eager, hungry mind state," he says in his book *Bomb the Suburbs*. "I'm trying to find the people no one has mobilized politically and bring them together." Political activists like Wimsatt hope to put hip-hop's self-expression and pride to good use.

Hip-Hop and Crime

Hip-hop gives voice to anyone and everyone who wants to use its style—and that means, of course, that not all rap lyrics are full of sweetness and light. Gangsta rap, which portrays an outlaw lifestyle of sex, drugs, and violence, has always been an important element of hip-hop. In 1988, when the first major album of gangsta rap, *Straight Outta Compton* by the rap group N.W.A (Niggaz With Attitude), was released, its violence generated controversy and outrage. The FBI even got involved—but attempts to censor gangsta rap just made it more famous, and both black and white kids paid even more attention to its new loud voice. NWA eventually became a platform for launching some of the most influential gangsta rappers, including Dr. Dre,

Rap music is not always pretty. But performers such as Dr. Dre (left, shown with Eminem at the Experience Music Project in 2000) would argue that the violent and misogynistic language common in gangsta rap simply reflects the world as they know it.

Ice Cube, and Eazy-E. Many people still hate the violent and the misogynistic (woman-hating) images in gangsta rap lyrics, but those who defend this style of music say that as ugly as it is, it is an accurate portrayal of America's inner-city life.

Hip-Hop and Religion

But if hip-hop gives crime and violence a voice, it also gives voice to a far different set of ideas. According to MTV.com, "pop culture is not only leaning toward religion—it's shouting about it. But one segment of the culture is shouting louder than everyone else: hip-hop." The

CAT POWER + JAMES BLUNT + BILLY JOEL

rollingstone.com
Issue 993 >> February 9, 2006 >> $3.95

Rolling Stone

BODE MILLER
Out of Control

GOD'S SENATOR
Inside the War Room of the Religious Right

BATTLESTAR GALACTICA
The Toughest, Smartest Show On Television

WILSON PICKETT
1941-2006

THE PASSION of KANYE WEST

Religion and spirituality are important to many rap stars. Some adopt a religious lifestyle, and others incorporate their spiritual beliefs into their music. Few, however, go as far as Kanye West, who posed as a Christ figure on the cover of *Rolling Stone.*

evidence is everywhere: hip-hop musician LL Cool J has plans to open a gospel-rap label; rap-gospel song "Lord You Know" is a top-ten hit; rapper DMX says he wants to "trade in his dog collar for a preacher's collar"; R. Kelly is putting out an entire album of inspirational hip-hop; and in Kanye West's song, "Jesus Walks," he pleads with God to stay by his side.

According to hip-hop legend P. Diddy, spirituality has always been present in hip-hop. "I always relate hip-hop to our old Negro spirituals," MTV.com quotes him as saying. He adds:

> **"They [spirituals] were sung in the cotton fields to help us get by, to help us not kill ourselves by going crazy [under] the worst oppression in the world. The music, the soulfulness, the spiritualness expressed in song helped us to get through another day. That's the same impact hip-hop has had on this generation. People could try to undermine it, but it's honestly the truth. Hip-hop has helped us make it through our life in the inner cities."**

Many modern churches see hip-hop as a powerful new vehicle for spreading the message of Christianity. As pastors seek to make urban churches multiethnic, they use dance, rap, and aerosol art to convey the message that ancient spirituality is still relevant to the modern world. Christianity is based on the teaching of Jesus Christ, who was himself a spokesperson for the downtrodden and the **marginalized**—and some **avant-garde** Christians dare to suggest that Jesus would have felt right at home delivering the Sermon on the Mountain in rap.

Hip-Hop and Fashion

Fashion is yet another way that hip-hop has crossed over all the old boundaries. In the 1990s, hip-hop fashion became "cool," and kids across America wore baggy pants, oversized rugby and polo shirts, and expensive sneakers. Today, inner-city hip-hoppers wear Tommy Hilfiger, Nautica, and Ralph Lauren, using the dress of upper-class whites as their statement of equality. These styles cut across ethnic groups; young people between the ages of twelve and twenty, whether they are black, white, Latino, or Asian, all tend to dress in the same hip-hop–influenced styles.

Hip-hop fashions influenced by rappers such as Jay-Z have crossed all economic and cultural barriers. On the first day of school in 2002, these Colorado Springs, Colorado, students showed off their hot trendy hip-hop–inspired outfits.

Hip-Hop and Social Activism

Hip-hop is a voice for everything from violence to **commercialism**, but despite its rage and brutal honesty, despite its willingness to make a buck, it has also always been a force for good. Ever since Afrika Bambaataa formed the Zulu Nation, hip-hop has consciously worked to use its strength to make the world a better place. Hip-hop artists as individuals donate their time and money to a variety of good causes, but perhaps the best and most organized social outreach for hip-hop is the Hip-Hop Summit Action Network (HSAN).

Founded in 2001 and run by hip-hop corporate mogul Russell Simmons (often referred to as the "Godfather of Hip-Hop"), the Hip-Hop Summit Action Network says in its mission statement:

> **"[HSAN] is dedicated to harnessing the cultural relevance of Hip-Hop music to serve as a catalyst for education advocacy and other societal concerns fundamental to the well-being of at-risk youth throughout the United States."**

The HSAN Web site (www.hsan.com) lists the following programs as its achievements:

- Sponsored more than forty successful Hip-Hop Summits in New York, Los Angeles, Detroit, Atlanta, Chicago, Houston, Miami, Washington, D.C., Kansas City, Philadelphia, Seattle, Birmingham and Dallas, providing a national template for engaging the Hip-Hop generation in community-building dialogues.

- On August 14, 2003, the Philadelphia Hip-Hop Summit registered over 11,000 voters, the largest number of young new voters registered ever at a single hip-hop event in the United States.

- On April 26, 2003, the Detroit Hip-Hop Summit mobilized over 17,000 youth participants at the Cobo Arena to commit to ongoing youth leadership development utilizing hip-hop.

- Fostered the establishment of grassroots Hip-Hop Summit Youth Councils in Queens, New York; Seattle, Washington; Baltimore, Maryland; Kansas City, Kansas; and Dallas, Texas. The Youth Councils engage youth in leadership development activities at a local level.

- Partnered with several other national organizations to effectively pursue shared program interests, including: the NAACP, National Urban League, Southern Christian Leadership Conference, and Rap the Vote on voter education and registration.

- Joined with the Alliance for Quality Education, mobilizing 100,000 New York City public school students and top hip-hop recording artists to a protest rally at City Hall which resulted in Mayor Bloomberg restoring $300 million in proposed cuts to the New York City public school budget. The National Federation of Teachers also partnered in this rally and, in part through the advocacy of the Hip-Hop community, they were able to finally negotiate a fair compensation contract for New York City public school teachers.

- Organized a public awareness campaign on the unfairness of the Rockefeller Drug Laws in New York culminating in a public rally of over 60,000.

- Worked in alliance with the Recording Industry Association of America (RIAA) in support of the Parental Advisory Label Program that alerts parents to explicit content in music.

- Defended Hip-Hop culture before members of the U.S. Congress and before federal regulatory agencies, including the Federal Trade Commission (FTC) and the Federal Communications Commission (FCC).

The HSAN also has a hip-hop reading program and works to promote literacy, freedom of speech, and economic advancement for at-risk youth throughout the United States.

"Hip-Hop Won't Stop: The Beat, The Rhymes, The Life"

In February 2006, the Smithsonian Institution announced the launch of "Hip-Hop Won't Stop: The Beat, The Rhymes, The Life," a new hip-hop exhibit to be created at the Smithsonian's National Museum of American History in Washington, D.C.

The project began with a news conference in New York City and a search for hip-hop artifacts. Rap stars, hip-hop artists, and producers who contributed items to the exhibit, including Ice-T and Russell

New Orleans Hip-Hop Summit on Financial Empowerment

Since its beginnings, hip-hop has reached out to help those in need. Here, HSAN receives the Campaign for Achievement award from Platform Learning in 2005. Shown left to right, David Lowenstein, Juan Torres, Dr. Benjamin Chavis, Rev. Run, Gene Wade, Russell Simmons, and Doug E. Fresh.

Simmons, said they were surprised to see the Smithsonian turn its attention to the three-decades-old art form. "It validates it," said Los Angeles–based rapper Ice-T. "It's a good feeling."

Other initial contributions to the museum's collection include a pair of turntables used by disc jockey Grandmaster Flash, known for the seminal 1982 hit "The Message," and a boom box owned by Fab 5 Freddy, the original host of *Yo! MTV Raps*, as well as pictures, album-cover artwork, and recordings.

Officials with the Smithsonian said the multi-year project will trace hip-hop from its origins in the 1970s to its status today, and it is estimated it will take three to five years before the exhibit will be ready for the public.

Fab 5 Freddy, Afrika Bambaataa, Brent D. Glass, Director of the Smithsonian Institution's Behring Center for American History, and DJ Kool Herc at a news conference in February 2006 in New York City. They are announcing the launch of "Hip-Hop Won't Stop: The Beat, The Rhymes, The Life," a new hip-hop exhibit in development at the Smithsonian's National Museum of American History in Washington, D.C.

The museum receives more than 80 percent of its money from the federal government and aims to represent the breadth of American culture. Its collections range from the early American flag which inspired the national anthem, to costumes and props from popular television shows; and now they include hip-hop turntables and boom boxes.

Conclusion

Hip-hop is far bigger than just rap music or its celebrities. Instead, when historians look back at the final decades of the twentieth century and the early twenty-first century, they may see hip-hop as this generation's "big idea" (the way that civil rights was the **baby boomers**' big idea). Whether people love hip-hop music or hate it, hip-hop's beat touches the way they see the world. It influences everything—from how we lace our shoes to what political candidates we vote for. What's more, it offers a cultural language that allows a black kid in Detroit to relate with an Asian kid in Hong Kong, a white kid in Beverly Hills with a Latino kid in Tijuana. As Russell Simmons says, "Racism still exists—but it is not strong enough to thwart the collective enjoyment of rap by youth in America and around the world."

Hip-hop activist William Upski Wimsatt summarized it well when he told the *San Francisco Chronicle*:

> **"We were talking about changing the world. Now we're doing it—through community organizing, electorial politics, business, media, art and philanthropy. Hip-hop gave us the tools, and now we're trying to build the house."**

1619 Slaves are first brought to the United States from Africa.

1920s Jazz becomes popular in the United States.

1933 James Brown, the "Godfather of Soul," is born.

1940s The blues combine with jazz to become rhythm and blues.

1970s DJ Kool Herc pioneers the use of breaks, isolations, and repeats using two turntables; Break dancing emerges at parties and in public places in New York City; Graffiti artist Vic makes his mark in New York, sparking the act of tagging; Hip-hop as a cultural movement begins in the Bronx, New York City.

1974 Hip-hop pioneer Afrika Bambaataa organizes the Universal Zulu Nation.

1976 Grandmaster Flash & the Furious Five pioneer hip-hop MCing and freestyle battles.

1982 Afrika Bambaataa introduces synthesizers and electric drum machine sounds on his album *Planet Rock*.

1984 *Graffiti Rock*, the first hip-hop television show, premieres.

1985 *Krush Groove*, a hip-hop film about Def Jam Recordings, is released featuring Run-D.M.C., Kurtis Blow, LL Cool J, and the Beastie Boys.

1986 Run-D.M.C. are the first rappers to appear on the cover of *Rolling Stone* magazine.

"(You Gotta) Fight for Your Right (To Party!)" by the Beastie Boys goes to the top ten on *Billboard* charts.

1988 *Yo! MTV Raps* premieres on MTV.

Annual record sales of hip-hop music reach $100 million.

Upper Hutt Posse releases *E Tu*, New Zealand's first album of pure hip-hop.

1989 First gangsta rap album is released by N.W.A.

Billboard adds rap charts to its magazines.

DJ Jazzy Jeff & The Fresh Prince become the first hip-hop artists to win a Grammy Award.

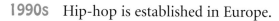
1990s   Hip-hop is established in Europe.

1992   Islamic Force releases its first single.

1996   Just D and Infinite Mass wins the Swedish version of the Grammys.

2001   Russell Simmons founds the Hip-Hop Summit Action Network.

2003   At the Detroit Hip-Hop Summit, over 17,000 youths commit to ongoing youth leadership development utilizing hip-hop on April 26.

2003   Over 11,000 voters are registered at the Philadelphia Hip-Hop Summit on August 14.

2004   National Hip-Hop Political Convention is held in Newark, New Jersey.

2005   Kanye West appears on the cover of *Time* magazine.

2006   Kanye West again up controversy when he is shown on the cover of *Rolling Stone* as Jesus.

       The Smithsonian Institution announces the launch of "Hip-Hop Won't Stop: The Beat, The Rhymes, The Life," a new hip-hop exhibit to be displayed at the Smithsonian's National Museum of American History in Washington, D.C.

2007   Grandmaster Flash and the Furious Five become the first rap artists inducted into the Rock and Roll Hall of Fame.

Books

Chang, Jeff. *Can't Stop, Won't Stop: A History of the Hip-Hop Generation.* New York: St. Martin's Press, 2005.

Jenkins, Sacha, Elliot Wilson, Chairman Jefferson Mao, Gabriel Alvarez, and Brent Rollins. *Ego Trip's Big Book of Racism.* New York: Regan Books, 2002.

Jenkins, Sacha, Elliot Wilson, Chairman Mao, Gabriel Alvarez, and Brent Rollins. *Ego Trip's Big Book of Rap Lists.* New York: St. Martins, 1999.

Kitwana, Bakari. *The Hip Hop Generation: Young Blacks and the Crisis in African American Culture.* New York: Basic Civitas Books, 2003.

Light, Alan, ed. *The Vibe History of Hip Hop.* New York: Three Rivers Press, 2001.

Nelson, George. *Hip-Hop America.* New York: Penguin, 2005.

Rose, Tricia. *Black Noise: Rap Music and Black Culture in Contemporary America.* Middletown, Conn.: Wesleyan University Press, 2004.

Toop, David. *Rap Attack 3: African Rap to Global Hip Hop.* London: Serpent's Tail, 2000.

Magazine Articles

Decurtis, Anthony. "Russell Simmons Speaks Out." *Rolling Stone,* September 13, 2001. www.rollingstone.com/news/story/5931521/russell_simmons_speaks_out.

Farley, Christopher John. "Let's Get Free." *Time,* March 27, 2000.

Farley, Christopher John. "Hip-Hop Nation." *Time,* February 8, 1999.

Hatch-Miller, Mark. "Everyday Struggle: A Conversation with Hip-Hop Historian Jeff Chang." *The Nation,* March 14, 2005.

Valby, Karen. "The Ego Has Landed." *Entertainment Weekly,* February 3, 2006.

Web Sites

Foundation of African Hiphop Culture Online
www.africanhiphop.com

Hip-hop.com
www.hip-hop.com/hiphop

Hip-Hop Summit Action Network
www.hsan.org

Muevelo hip-hop ezine (in Spanish)
www.muevelohiphop.com

National Hip-Hop Political Convention
www.hiphopconvention.org

SOHH
www.sohh.com

activist—someone who vigorously and sometimes aggressively pursues a political or social goal.

advocacy—active verbal support for a cause or position.

agenda—an underlying personal motive.

alienation—a feeling of being isolated or withdrawn or of not belonging or sharing in something.

avant-garde—artistically new, experimental, or unconventional.

baby boomers—those who were born between 1946 and 1964.

bootleg—created illegally.

civil rights movement—the political and social campaign of the 1950s and 1960s for the rights that all citizens of a society are supposed to have.

collage—a combination of different things.

commercialism—excessive emphasis on profit-making.

conservatives—those reluctant to change, preferring the status quo.

consumerism—an attitude that values the acquisition of material goods.

Depression—the worldwide period of severe economic decline and mass unemployment that lasted from 1929 until 1939.

emceeing—acting as master of ceremonies.

fusions—the blendings of musical styles or elements from more than one tradition.

genre—one of the categories into which artistic works can be divided into on the basis of form, style, or subject matter.

grassroots—the ordinary people of a community or organization, as opposed to the leadership.

innovations—new ideas or methods.

institution—an established law, custom, or practice.

liberals—people who are tolerant of different views and standards of behavior in others, and favor reform that extend democracy and protect individual freedoms.

marginalized—prevented from having attention or power.

philanthropy—a desire to improve humanity through charitable activities.

philosophical—relating to the study of the nature of life and reality.

platinum—in music, singles that have sold more than one million copies or CDs that have sold two million.

Polynesian—someone who was born or raised on any of the islands of the central and southern Pacific.

secular—not controlled by a religious organization or concerned with religious or spiritual matters.

segregated—kept apart, often because of race or ethnicity.

sovereignty—freedom from outside interference.

spontaneous—unplanned.

subculture—a separate social group within a larger culture and that usually has ideas and practices that differ from those of the larger group.

testimony—the public profession of faith.

Rosa Waters has a degree in creative writing, and has written for various publications. She has worked in an inner-city crisis center, so she knows firsthand some of the challenges urban youth face. Although she makes no claim to musical talent of her own, her husband is active in the music scene, and the interface between creativity and culture is one of her ongoing interests.

Picture Credits

page

2: KRT/NMI
8: Reuters/Mike Hutchings
11: PictureArts/OBrien Productions
12: KRT/NMI
15: WENN Photos
17: NMI
18: KRT/NMI
20: KRT/NMI
23: PRNewsFoto/NMI
25: Catuffe/SIPA
26: KRT/NMI
28: Tsuni/iPhoto
31: NMI

33: Reuters/Mark Cardwell
34: NMI
36: Kazuhiro Nogi/AFP/Getty Images
38: KRT/NMI
39: Lydie/SIPA
41: KRT/NMI
42: Ciro Cesar/La Opinion
44: Zuma Press/Nancy Kaszerman
47: KRT/Nancy Stone
48: WENN
50: KRT/Mark Reis
53: PRNewsFoto/NMI
54: WireImage/Jemal Countess

Front cover: (top left) CAPS; (top right)Piotr Redlinski/Sipa Press; (bottom left) Reuters/Mike Blake; (bottom right)BSIP/Jack Griffin